This Twinkl Originals book belongs to:

_____

_____

Listen and follow...

1 Scan the QR code using the camera on your phone or tablet. (You might need to download a QR reader first.)

2 Click on the link that pops up.

3 Press play to hear the story being read aloud.

4 Turn the page when you hear the twinkle!

First published 2021 © Twinkl Ltd of Wards Exchange, 197 Ecclesall Road, Sheffield S11 8HW

ISBN: 978-1-914331-28-2

MIX
Paper from responsible sources
FSC® C022913

We're passionate about giving our children a sustainable future, which is why this book is made from Forest Stewardship Council® certified paper. Learn how our Twinkl Green policy gives the planet a helping hand at www.twinkl.com/twinkl-green.

Printed in the United Kingdom.

10 9 8 7 6 5 4 3 2 1

A catalogue record for this book is available from the British Library.

Twinkl is a registered trademark of Twinkl Ltd.

A Twinkl ORIGINAL

Around the World with Max and Lemon

twinkl

Twinkl Educational Publishing

Max was in her tent drawing a picture of Lemon. "There are no other toys that look like you, Lemon," she said.

Dad popped his head inside. "That's because Lemon is unique!"

"What does 'unique' mean?" Max asked.

"It means 'one of a kind'," said Dad. "We are all unique. There's no one exactly like you!"

"Not even up a mountain?" asked Max.

"Not even in the desert or the jungle," said Dad.

"Not even in the Arctic or the ocean?" asked Max.

"Not even on a faraway island!" said Dad. "You could travel the whole world and not find a single person who is exactly the same as you. You are unique."

"Hmm, I'm not sure," said Max. "Come on, Lemon. Let's find out for ourselves."

Max packed a rucksack with everything that she and Lemon would need.

She waved goodbye to Mum and Dad, then headed off on her scooter to find out if she really was one of a kind.

On a tall mountain, Max made a friend called Anka, who loved bright colours.

"Just like me!" said Max. "Do you like to do colourful paintings?"

But Anka preferred to weave colourful patterns.

"We're similar... but not the same," smiled Max, giving Anka a special picture that she had drawn.

She said goodbye to her new friend and headed on her way.

In a dry desert, Max made a friend called Noor, who loved music.

"Just like me!" said Max. "Do you like to sing?"

But Noor preferred to play lovely tunes on her favourite instrument.

"We're similar... but not the same," smiled Max, giving Noor a special picture that she had drawn.

She said goodbye to her new friend and headed on her way.

In a thick jungle, Max made a friend called Pakaya, who loved stories.

"Just like me!" said Max. "Do you like to read them in books?"

But Pakaya preferred to listen to tales sung by his dad.

"We're similar... but not the same," smiled Max, giving Pakaya a special picture that she had drawn.

She said goodbye to her new friend and headed on her way.

In the cold Arctic, Max made a friend called Gertrude, who loved the snow.

"Just like me!" said Max. "Do you like to whizz down hills on a sledge?"

But Gertrude preferred to go snowshoeing.

"We're similar... but not the same," smiled Max, giving Gertrude a special picture that she had drawn.

She said goodbye to her new friend and headed on her way.

In the blue ocean, Max made a friend called Adam, who loved to swim.

"Just like me!" said Max. "Do you like to float on the surface?"

But Adam preferred to dive deep down under the water.

"We're similar... but not the same," smiled Max, giving Adam a special picture that she had drawn.

She said goodbye to her new friend and headed on her way.

On a faraway island, Max made a friend called Chloe, who loved animals.

"Just like me!" said Max. "Do you like penguins best?"

But Chloe's favourite animal was the enormous humpback whale.

"We're similar... but not the same," smiled Max, giving Chloe a special picture that she had drawn.

She said goodbye to her new friend and headed on her way.

Once Max had ticked off every place on her list, she started the journey home.

Pacchanta

Sinai

Tari Basin

Alaska

Sabah

Tristan da Cunha

It wasn't long before she was
back with her family.

"How was your trip?" asked Dad. "Did you find anyone exactly like you?"

"I made lots of new friends," said Max. "Each one was a bit like me, but no one was exactly the same."

"So, you travelled the **whole** world and didn't find a single person exactly like you?" asked Dad.

"I guess I am unique after all!" smiled Max. "Just like everybody else!"

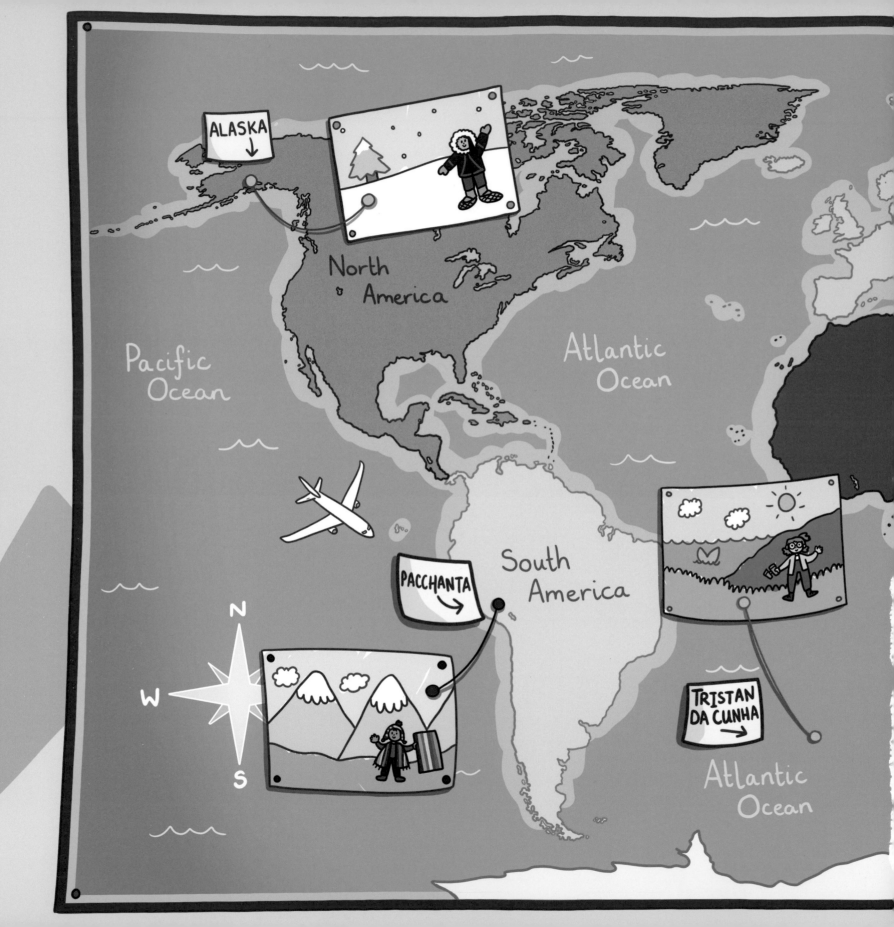

Welcome to the world of Twinkl Originals!

Buy extra copies of Originals stories in our online shop!

Board books for ages 0-3

Let's Name the Colours

Let's Go to the Farm!

Let's Take a Trip!

Picture books for ages 3-7

The Bear who Came to Babysit

Doris the Loris

Longer stories for ages 7-11

Leila and the Gods

PHYLLIS AND THE FOSSIL FINDERS

twinkl Book Club

Books delivered to your door

Enjoy original works of fiction in beautiful printed form, delivered to you each half term and yours to keep!

1 Join the club at twinkl.com/book-club.

2 Enter your delivery address and choose your book type.

3 Enjoy a brand new book, every half term!

twinkl ORIGINALS

The Twinkl Originals app

Now, you can read Twinkl Originals stories on the move! Enjoy a broad library of Twinkl Originals eBooks, fully accessible offline.

Download on the App Store   GET IT ON Google Play

Search 'Twinkl Originals' in the App Store or on Google Play.